For Peter,
this copy of

Burning the Old Year

"only our luminous days
will stay with us."
It was great meeting
you in Durango!
un abrazo de,
steven
october, 1989

STEVEN F. WHITE

Burning
the
Old
Year

1984
Greensboro, North Carolina
Unicorn Press, Inc.

Grateful acknowledgement is made to the editors and publishers of the following periodicals where some of these poems appeared:

> *Aspen Anthology, International Poetry Review, La Prensa Libre* (San José, Costa Rica), *La Prensa Literaria* (Managua, Nicaragua), *Northwest Review Books, Porch.*

The image *Cassis* on the cover is copyright © 1984 by the artist, Arthur Secunda. *All rights reserved.*

Library of Congress Cataloging in Publication Data

White, Steven F., 1955-
  Burning the old year.

  I. Title.
PS3573.H47478B8   1984   811'.54   83-27430
ISBN 0-87775-159-5
ISBN 0-87775-160-9 (pbk.)

Unicorn Press, Inc.
Post Office Box 3307
Greensboro, NC 27402

Table of Contents

I

II

III

I

Esto que escribo
nace
de mis viajes a las inmovilidades del pasado.

Roberto Sosa

Slaughterhouse

My people are blind
to ghost-ridden days
and coffins moving
full-sailed up a purple river.
They take off their shoes
and fall asleep
under the spell of television.
In their dreams they tear
the black flag down, burn it,
and raise their own colors.
But what if they wake up
tomorrow, thinking
of coffee, and come face to face
with another life
as customary as their own?

Constellations they have never seen
will grace the sky of their new world.
Then, beginning at dawn after market,
they will lead dumb brutes
into a room of high windows
where the floor steams
with a wealth of blood.
While one beast's throat is slit,
another kicks out its life
and still another is hoisted
toward the ceiling on clanking chains.

Rush hour traffic in Chicago.
Barrels of fly-covered heads.
The two worlds are one.
I am being
collected in slippery buckets
by boys red with me,
barefoot and laughing.

Riobamba, Ecuador

11

First Class

The train stopped.
He looked up:
another nameless village
on the way to Puno.
The vendors surged around
the silence
of the first class car.
Soon someone was tapping
the glass. He opened
his guide to South America.
The train lurched.
A woman ran
along the platform,
laughing as the train
departed. Oranges
fell from her basket.
The bloody sheep's head
she lifted toward him
disappeared, reappeared
in window after window.

The Angels in Quito

When you wake, your patron saint, the apparition of the lady in the clouds, is beside your bed. She knows you, lives with you like a golden-haired parasite boring into your heart. She dresses you in the same clothes you have always worn—the layers of skirts, the bright sweater and the shawl. When she places the dusty felt hat on your head like a crown, she touches your face so lightly that it tingles in expectation.

You wish today were Sunday, because on Sundays the frequency of bells makes your future seem so beautiful that it begins to peal inside you. But today, like most days, the uncertainty is unbearable. The afternoon rain from clouds that cannot empty themselves drives you away from the waiting with your mangos.

So you walk up the street with your fruit on your back. You pass the blue stalls of trinkets and religious amulets and wonder if your guardian is still with you. You climb the stairs that are worn and brown like the many hands that built them. You see clusters of people in the plaza in front of San Francisco—your church, your home.

Inside, where the paint from a saint's face litters the floor with flakes of gold, you kneel and pray to Zapa Inca. And then, because you are the mother of five dead children whose mouths are filled with dust, you take your votive candle before the shrine of your lady in the clouds. Here, you are separated from her by a pane of glass. The glass is your paper, the candle your white crayon. You scribble your message in faith. You pass the candle over your face, rub the magic into your hair, and make the sign of the cross. Your coin is in the box and the candle will burn all night.

You leave, the stone floor as hard as your bare feet. You shuffle slowly past the paintings of the old prophets effaced by darkness and take the first step outside the church where the gray light of heaven has been waiting like a bird of prey. In the distance you see the white angels, towels wrapped around their heads, their bodies misshapen with strength and burdened with huge sacks of flour for the next day's bread. Amen.

Mass in a Town Called Chinchero

While giant chicha jugs wobbled
with laughter outside the church,

a woman knelt on stone.

She bowed her head so the priest
could create Christ in Quechua.

When the host disappeared
like the moon above the fields,
the image was almost human:

I saw him stride in the light
of the stained glass.
He wore a straw hat against the sun
and a poncho good for life.

He shouldered his plow like a rifle
and in his right hand raised
a fistful of golden wheat.

Prayer

¡Salud! ¡Y sufre!
C. V.

Let your fierce ghost rest, please, Vallejo,
¡porque me estás sacando el pellejo!

The Day of the Dead

la muerte extendió los sueños
en vez de la firmeza de su rostro
Eliseo Diego

ack every year to find my face.
to lie down in the picnic they bring
watch the sunlight braid the children's hair.
an I never knew squats on a grave
e ground that welcomed her family
es below the folds of her skirts.

re here with us, she prays.
ear us. Even though your voice
xed with wind, we still see it.

t I do not eat I leave behind
e I have no life and cannot die.

h year it is the same.
mfort my face and go;
cheated and the weak keep living;
d the dogs tip wicker baskets
nong freshly painted stones.

Calderón, Ecuador

17

Our Father

Deliver us from these peaks
that breathe the dust we are.
Deliver us from these canyons
that swallow the sun and the rain.
Deliver us from this straw hut
and the smoke of every meal.
Deliver us from the bones
of our children,
this plow, this empty sack.
Deliver us from the womb
where your tiny face lived
until all this death was born.

Messenger

I have lost the sun. It is noon
and the sky billows with black sails.
My people are buried under rocks and trees.
The mountain of death is holy
because it is filled with a love
I cannot understand.

I raise my hand to say goodbye.
My horse snorts at the mystery
in the air. Soon the wind will erase
the marks of hooves in ash.

The minutes swallow me
the way the ash falls, gently
covering my fields, my village
and the still bodies of my family.

The black wind will guide me to the mountain.

The Harpist

While the day rattles over the cobbled
streets of Ayacucho, this harp watches
the world for me. Each of its strings
is a river of Peru.
Song after song, tear after tear.
Friends give me bread
because I make them cry.

I count the arches of memory.
Soon I will be in my place
like everything I cannot see.
Time buzzes around the sweet fruit
in the market: yesterday the wad
of *coca* I spit into the morning
and tomorrow looking at me
the way my eyes burn holes in the sky.

Play, hands, before the silence
takes us apart.

The music flows from ten horizons
across the empty, high plain
and someone sobs in the plaza.

When the Dreamers Saw the Ruins

"Vuelven los dioses" dijo Moctezuma
José Emilio Pacheco

In the smoking mirror
of a lake. There was no mistake.
Their minds, clear as the wind.
There were the fields on fire.
There were the empty sockets of homes
and the temples that gave
shape to their builders.
The serpent of laughter
multiplied on faces of stone.
The sun sang to splintered
bone as the new sickness
sailed from the lips of the sea.
They heard the red tiger of the rain
say goodbye to the paths
of water where it walked.
They felt the passage
of every moon and year
and watched the blood
that finally reaches
its place of peace.
As they read the night
by firelight,
the dreamers filled with fear,
slowly,
the way the sky
was revealing its stars.
They witnessed
their death at the hands
of the king who disowned them,
the beasts unleashed
across the land they loved,
and rivers of gold
flowing through ruined cities.

El Arrayán

for Holger

Ay, ay ay que cueca tan sola baila
el huaso chileno en la noche negra.
Armando Rubio

Sand-charged winds, icebergs
and a darkness in Chile
some call peace.
But sleep is still besieged by
the hum of factories,
the clang of pans when the rich
had to wait their turn for bread,
the cry of the eyeless body
that stared beyond the stadium,
and footsteps in the depths of *La Moneda*.
Those days when tanks rolled
around the corner instead of buses
have disappeared like black widows
inside the walls of the mansion.

The Southern Cross sails the sky
above your stone house in El Arrayán
toward the lit sliver of Santiago in the west.
This isn't the last place on earth, nor is it
the only place you need to go. But at least
here the natural course of time is clearer.
You and Sergio have been planting trees
(peumo, pimiento, espino, quillay)
to reforest these arid mountains.
The newspapers say that after five years
the curfew has been lifted.
Nobody knows exactly
how long anything lasts now
or even if these new trees will grow.

Santiago, Chile

The Quinta Heren

Las enfermedades tienen una madre...
José María Arguedas

A woman named Piedad owns a world in Peru
that is lost in Lima. It's small—
just a handful of old mansions
surrounded by walls and gates of iron—
the way a world should be. She lives
there with portraits of her family.

Things have changed. Hearts of solid gold
no longer beat behind the gaunt façades.
Wet clothes hang from windows like tongues,
armies of caterpillars devour the trees
and smoke from barricaded streets
floats past the statues of marble.

She wanders with the last light
and listens for the clop of horses,
the carriages clattering home.
She waits for the man who lights the lamps,
while her armed servants, silence within silence,
pass through the black paper of her night.

II

Tengo que hacer algo con el lodo de la historia, cavar en
el pantano y desenterrar la luna
de mis padres.

Pablo Antonio Cuadra

Old Glory

While we're talking in the rain
by a spring river that will outlive us,
a hand reaches from the future
searching for what we were.
It finds a flag and follows
a long, red thread
until it reaches the mouth
of a river of blood. A woman
gathers her wet clothes there
and runs from the sun
that pulses with helicopters.
She is from a country
where the cities and streets
will soon be renamed.
Through trenches, smoke
and human flames,
a hand reaches from the future
and touches a flag where a woman runs
along white roads rutted by jeeps.
She runs toward the house where she died,
where her shadow remains on the wall.
Our conversation goes on in the rain.
A woman appears before us screaming
from another world, this world,
from the silence of the past.
She has made up her mind to live.
A hand reaches from the future,
finds a flag
and rips the stars from the sky.

Tyranny

The suns of all my days are amassing
on the horizon and now, less vital
than love, pull me from your embrace
toward a sky incinerating its past.

The suns of all my days circle my waist.
By what right destroy this solar plexus
or leave to live the liberty of death?
Frightened wheel of nerves, I recede in light

so dark you can feel the distance between our hands.

Epicenter

Resounding rain falls from the sole
dark window of the night
because I beat
inside the same black glass.
It is how I lift my crystal hands
with the windwracked hair of *palmas*
bowed by dust for months
to receive this war in good faith.

On what sand did I crawl
from the sea? On what city of smoke
would my cold eyes open?
The bullet that shatters me
will beat inside
my blood then lodge
in a place more comfortable
that is harder and has no conviction:

up here, past the sharpshooter's burnt window.

León

The jeeps circle beneath the steeple of *El Calvario*.
The profligate army advances ill at ease
in the tropical sun: the city of León is only theirs by day.
The people have learned from the dead
 a new language for the rooftops at night.

While in my dreams
I make love with a woman dressed in flames
and the black gloves of fear,

di Chirico's streets outside are filling
with an emptiness that fingers all the locked doors.
The metal voices wake me and I shudder.
On the patio a parrot is crying like a child
who has forfeited his home forever.

Masters of Lightning

for *los muchachos* in Matagalpa

Fue bárbara y primitive
pero poética.
Ernesto Cardenal

Masters of lightning,
throw yourselves down on the streets!
The splinters will be yours!
The ashes will be yours!
The city, yours!
Let the faces be blank
to the marksman's blinding eye!
Four points of flesh and bone
of elbows and knees
that weigh so heavily on the sphere,
masters of lightning,
throw yourselves down on the streets!

The Lightning

for Carlos Martínez Rivas

Invent your own sky.
Make it infernal, transparent
for the poets who follow you like birds
flying toward panes of glass. Every bottle
in the world is yours. Don't worry.
When your last phantom has risen in the rain
and the guanacaste tree has sunk its roots deep in your eyes,
when the city of syringes,
when the veins of black blood,
when the mother,
when the white vulture of your words,
when the *¡Ay, Rubén!*,
when everything falls in the night
and is swallowed drop by drop . . .

The lightning flickered across your forehead.
Hendecasyllables. Anvils of light!

The Children of War

Somos la orquídea del acero
Joaquín Pasos

The children of war sing with ashen hair
and cannot relive the ingenuous games
after the alchemy of the heart.
The future Achilles, ingot of gold,
stared from the river of his mother's palm
at her other hand leaving him vulnerable.

Abandoned to love, nothing they know is
stronger than the clenching of tiny fists.

Easter in Estelí

No hand rolled back stone from the cryptic dawn.
The miracle was streets of blood instead.
My born rage burned beneath towers of gone.
All that had risen was smoke from the dead.

Insurrection

*"Too long a sacrifice
can make a stone of the heart."*
W. B. Yeats

Umbrellas in Costa Rica. Rain
strafes the park where I walk.
Bronze angels feast
on the dead whose mouths
are the black zeros of wars
no one remembers.

After the bells in every town
and the dancing in all the streets,
what will save Nicaragua
from the empty blow of tomorrow?
The living stream must keep its guns
and sing red lullabies to its children.

The war continues beating in my chest.
To survive means never to forget.
I will take the solitary insurrection home.

San José, Costa Rica

Reconstruction

His country: he saw its walls
destroyed because he said so.
Before daybreak the tyrant fled
with his father's ashes cradled
in his arms. The flames waved goodbye
saying *We will find you and your son.*
Everywhere his image toppled and burned.
As the black heralds receded in the sky,
the dead were lowered underground
in the crates that had arrived with guns.

There is a song on all the scarred lips
and already the people furrow
the forehead of the beast
to reclaim the land.
But they are startled because their eyes
find nothing that does not recall
the absence of death.

You Left Us the Sun

In memory of Joaquín Pasos

Joaquín, you left us the sun:
an astonished sun of peace
that watches a sun of war
lift its head on the horizon.
Joaquín, you left us the river:
the torrent of images you rode
in your hammock as it swayed
like a drunken boat.

I have a distant memory of you,
without wings,
without light,
without blood.
You are staring into the silence
at the heart of some trees
on the far bank of the river
where the current bends,
where a liquid shoulder
slides over a cemetery of mud,
where the end of one life
is simply the beginning
of another, a farewell
to the light that scarred
the turbulent waters of your time.
You were right.
The wound is long, from here to the sea!

Joaquín, you left us a road in the air.
The darker the road we are,
the more intensely we desire
light that blinds, that burns
inside us, because we remember
how time will eat the color of our eyes.

Joaquín, you left us a gust
of brilliant birds. The *chocoyos*
cry in the sky: yellow, green, green,
yellow, turning in the sky's open eye.

At night, after the sun had sunk
in the red pages of history
and the petals of your days were at your feet,
you went out to hunt the stars with a rifle.
The people of your country have built
a coffin of shadows for the tyrant.
Did you hear their song of war even then?
That swift blade of light
in the country of thunder?

Joaquín, you left us a rope of dreams.
Our empty bucket descends in silence.
If there are angels down here,
their cries will not wake us.

Joaquín, you left us the future.
Tomorrow flares in the distance
as yesterday remains inside us
in the embers of memory.
Joaquín, you left us the sun.
Each day it rises
we have our chance to retell history.
It sang for you, Joaquín.
The whistle of death.
Were you looking too far
into the past or the future
that day when the iguana
peered in your window to mock you?

Nicaragua

The sun was black.
Now it burns like gold.
Soldiers circled the sun.
We killed them.
We are the angels
who clear the rubble.
We are the angels
who rebuild the cities.
We are the people of Nicaragua.
For the first time,
a wishbone of light
stretches across the land.
We know the plow
will always uncover more bones,
but our work
neither begins nor ends
with any birth or death.
Our power comes to us
as the wind came to the trees
of Sandino's mountains.
We are the angels
who flower and burn.
We are the people of Nicaragua.

III

. . . with a belief that became
but small light
in the breadth of time where we began
among each other, where we lived
in the hour farthest from God.

Carolyn Forché

The Bright Wings:
from Nicaragua to Oregon

for Nancy

You are not one of those creatures
looking for a form and a way
into one realm from another realm.
I am. And no matter how far we walk
in these mountains and trees of ice
I can't explain it to you.
I take off my gloves.
I show you my hands.
You can't see them flickering
with the war. I place your hand
against my face. You can't feel
the walls pocked with gunfire.
I run my fingers through your hair
but the sun is still tropical.
You kiss me in the cold air
but my eyes are still the clocks
frozen in their steeple by earthquakes.
Below us, the winter fog snakes
with the creek and a plume of smoke
rises from our chimney. We follow
the logging road until we reach the snow.
I want to be here completely,
with the clouds of our breath as we climb,
with the silence and the trees
that watch us pass, with the flakes
of gold in the water and snow in the air,
with the wind that inhabits the arch
of this morning, with the wood
that must be stacked and split by our door,
with the animals that must be fed,
with our good neighbors,
with the language we invented
that is easier for us to speak each day,
and with the bright wings that open
and close the night as we dream together.
A patch of ice cracks under my feet.
We embrace. You hold me here.

43

Oregon

Oregon is difficult to translate,
when not a single road leads home.
My heart hides in my chest
like an owl waiting in a hollow tree.
Tonight my insomniac will leave me,
wing out over the smoldering kingdom
and scan the shadows to survive.
She will be there. She has smoothed
a place for herself, slipped from her dress
and stretched out, vulnerable
among the moonlit weeds.

The scream of the late
train to Portland . . . Someone
I know—the distant part of me,
the silhouette leaning against
a lurching square of darkness—
hears the music of the rails,
watches the city sink under wave
upon wave of black mountains,
sits back with the Thunderbird
between his thighs, then lifts
the bottle slowly toward his lips
and calls the world good night.

The Long Rain

The long rain is no longer but not yet.
Help me bless the weather for what it knows.
My sleep is no one's, my dreams are unmet.

There breathe oblivion's fields at sunset
where an unseen river of diamond flows.
The long rain is no longer but not yet.

Armed shadows stand guard on the parapet.
I rise with herons and plummet from crows.
My sleep is no one's, my dreams are unmet.

This waiting is like a blind man's regret
who seeks the sun in chambers of a rose.
The long rain is no longer but not yet.

Teach me to read the sky's palm and forget
how, parched and patient, the nightmare grows.
My sleep is no one's, my dreams are unmet.

I live to match my storms alone but let
lightning flash inside your heart of windows.
The long rain is no longer but not yet.
My love is no one's, my love is unmet.

Marcela

When you have buried
your fear and foolish hopes,
listen for her in the mountains
where she talks with the streams.
Watch for her at night:
the fire in the distance
will not burn you,
the sword shining far away
will not cut you.
Recognize her for what she is:
the mystery that flows
in everything she has been before,
an arc joining all ages,
a particle, a pulse
greeting itself across time.
You see the light of the dying
return to the sky
and wish she would hold you
over the fire and burn away your death.
But she sails into the future
under the colors
of her own republic.
She will never love you.

The Wheel

1

Even the birds have abandoned you
as if they had finished scattering your bones.
But you found her shadow
that is the color of your blood.
She is holding the wheel of the seasons
and speaks in an opaque voice. She is inside
that tree, the one with flowers like white bells.
They open and wither and fall at the same time
because they know the night cannot contain them.

She wants to help you return
across the bridges that were blown away.

2

The orchard was in bloom! Apple trees!
Clouds of petals spinning
in a dizzying sky as you floated
on your back with her, naked in the pond.
Spring jolted and rolled into summer
like a train that would not stop.
A green wave ascended the mountains
and everything seemed at peace but you.

3

She watched you as you both slept in autumn
and the forest was in flames. You did not
smell her in the cold air that night when she
froze you with a shaft of light.
The shot sang. You saw a puff of smoke
from the invisible gun just as your eyelids
flickered open with hers. Only the vague
image of a buck leaping over branches
as she kissed you and went back to sleep.

4

You made love with her in the eye of winter.
Outside, the weightless snow doubled
and cracked the spines of trees and buried
the house like a seed the spring would never find.
The next morning, you waded in the snow.
Crows crossed a sky of steel
above the frozen waterfall inside you.
In the needles of the air, you knew
she would conduct storm after storm
with the wind in her hands.

5

The rain tastes like her and fills the rivers
and the tree sways with her voice. And bells!
Let the stars and moon bloom! Let the bones bloom!
Let the sun, petal by giant petal, fall from the sky!
Let her sink in your blood with her flowers!

Vermont. A red house. The clouds in her basket.
She is waving on the hill of all the seasons.

Progress

Here are my blueprints and maps.
I am progress. I live inside you:
a current of air, of water
of light leaving clouds,
of darkness and of me
flowing from memory to memory.
Oil, timber, uranium, coal.
The land, the sky and the seas are mine.
I am progress.
My country's fist will never open
and bloom.

Poem to a Foreign Country

All day long, the sunflowers had followed
the explosions at the center of the sun.
I couldn't sleep last night.
The people of my country can't
feel the darkness twist inside them.
They think they're still in control
even though everything smells
like money. What they bought is rising
over the White House: a wheel spinning
in a wheel, and an eagle with the hands
of a man under its wings.

Perhaps those who are in power believe
that they can watch their sculptures of fire
destroy the planet from a safe place
without dying like the rest of us.
Perhaps they think the cataract of ash
will not touch the ones who are important.
I hear the sun call the next day
like an orphan lost on the streets of some nightmare.
Maybe those who would trade our eyes
for more precious stones love us so much
that they will extinguish our future by kissing it.

I couldn't sleep last night.
The dead were busy pushing their flowers
through the unlit corridors
that are the pores of my skin.
The curtains in my bedroom filled with wind.
The President flew to another country.
Peasants walked in a long line
up the face of a mountain.
I couldn't sleep last night.
I kept thinking about the betrayal of my people.
The bombs were drifting toward the earth.

I looked up and saw sunflowers bend toward me.
The great seeds spilled from their faces.
The earth shuddered. It would have to begin again.

A Sign of Summer

Solitude is the age of the sun:
the blackberries fall to the earth,
the corn grows until it tassels
into a sky of wind and color
and clouds bringing cooler
weather. Solitude is the sun
coming of age, the ripeness
that we live by, the power
of maturing until we fall
as old as the sun in the
solitude of our age. We
grow and walk against the sky
on a ridge whipped by wind
and we feel the themes of seasons
repeat themselves. We grow and
fall into the sun, never freer
as in this solitude, and a dream
of dreaming all this music together.

The River We Love

Now the last leaves spin below passing birds
and the wind blows through the spokes
of another season turning in us and in the trees
and in the river at our feet. Tell me,
when winter tosses the sun's head
into its cart of cold rain,
that we will find a way to keep warm.
If you carry the burning cipher in your eyes
and if you believe that at the center
of your voice is a fire. I will rise
from those eyes and that voice.

Peace in us, peace on Earth. Tomorrow
our planet may be as dead as the moon.
If I tell you I love you, it is because I want
to feel the sky breathe with all its might
into my lungs. The river we love crashes
to the coast where winter approaches whale by whale.
It eats its own banks, crests, and will wash away our place
like memory. It has all the time in the world.
I kiss your lips, your neck and your breasts
and enter the black flame of your sex
because it is the only way I have
of knowing your shape encircled by its own light.

Each moment of time is a fire, the voice of life,
small enough to pour from my hands to yours.
Even though you have touched each of my faces,
you won't know me until we learn to breathe
a stream of faces in unison. Then suddenly
we remember the power to heal
each other in our changes, the changes of the world
and everything outside lies within:

a new landscape where all this water
flows with a part of us beyond death.
When the terrible weapons
begin to glow inside us,
we will be lost in a greater light.

The men who dream of having metal bodies
say war is beautiful
which means war is good
business. Someday soon
our headless bodies may float past
the eyes of their soldiers.
"No one knows us," you whisper
by the river we love.

Perhaps, for a while, you will confuse me with someone else
when your blood collides with the blood
of another lover in the dark passages
of your sleep. But think of me as a poplar,
the thinnest tree, and that I am the one
who absorbed your blood through my roots.
Or imagine me walking the shoreline
of your skin and that our promise
is building near the horizon like a wave.
It's not enough to live
and die beneath this weak sun.
But it frightens me to speak
of things beyond my strength.

A child kneels in me by a stream
surrounded by mountains.
The water that opens his hands
holding the smooth, white stones

will reach us many times
by the river we love. The years
will turn us back,
against the current,
to our first voices.
The child climbs higher in my memory,
upstream,
to the place where it bubbles
from two holes in the ground
and sees the sun for the first time.

Please don't let anyone steal the light from your eyes.
When we are apart, let's lead simple lives
so there is time to dream
about the smell of each other's hair
and the long curve of our bodies together.
Leave room for my face in the future—
a small candle burning against whatever you can't control.
Our words existed before our tongues.
Our blood signaled to the sky before we were born.
Today, beside the river we love, my life
is honeycombed with your mystery
as if you had returned with pollen from the sun.
Who can see us, the twin constellations,
as we fall through each other and
move with the day across a blue field of light?

The Constellations of History

One nation holds a gun
on another to punish itself
and I wonder why I love you.
One generation fails the next,
the children destroy themselves for revenge
and I wonder why I love you.
The pain that makes me human
makes me hate myself
as if I were someone else
and I wonder why I love you.
No more islands of safety
in this wilderness of flags—
there is no ground that hasn't tasted blood.
And I wonder why I love you.

When we are alone with death
and the constellations of history,
when we feel ourselves
lowered by a rope into that sky,
only our luminous days will stay with us.
We align ourselves with the skies
of other ages where change was possible
and realize that it was no treason
to love most what we might have done.
If we failed, we will guide the next
navigators as they create their future
against what was and shall be,
against what was and shall be no more.
And I wonder why I love you.

Burning the Old Year

for Daniel

No se enteraron los hombres.
Solo tú y yo, Ceniciento.
Rafael Alberti

The eucalyptus smoke rising to meet
the future: I still remember the fires
of New Year's Eve like so many eyes in Quito
just before you vanished into Colombia.

We followed the custom exactly.
We made the figure of straw.
I dressed *el año viejo*
in our old clothes and you
soaked it with gasoline.

Then we placed it
on an altar of branches
in the street. You threw
the match at midnight.

It was like burning
all the selves except the one
that leaps over the flames
into the new year.

I have no idea what became of you,
nor do I need to know. But I think
of that night and what I was then.
Only you and I can understand
all the things that are ash.

A Question of Time

A trireme! Our country lit
by whitecaps, powered by hands
that crack and bleed on millions
of oars. Above our shackles and stench,
beyond our breath,
the sky must be blue.

The empire has ended. We row
with nowhere to go and not a friend
in the world to turn to. So they
whip us harder, and harder still
until I almost lose
the dazzling coast of justice
that shimmers behind my eyelids.

Give us to the sharks cried a voice
when the great guards passed last night.
They will, as soon as we reach
warmer waters.

A woman beside me asks if I think
she is a ghost. I kill a spider
on her cheek and say nothing.

No one sees this black sail bound for war.
No one feels the coming rain
of fire and the riptide of blood
across the decks.
No one whispers mutiny.

But I do.

Biographical Note

Steven F White was born in Abington, Pennsylvania in 1955 and was raised in Glencoe, Illinois. He received a B.A. in English from Williams College and an M.A. in Spanish and Hispanic American literature from the University of Oregon. His awards include the Academy of American Poets Prize in 1975 and 1977 as well as the Hubbard Hutchinson Fellowship from Williams College which enabled him to travel and to work in various Latin American countries for two years. His poems and translations have appeared in numerous magazines including REVIEW *(Center for Inter-American Relations),* NEW DIRECTIONS ANTHOLOGY, NICARAGUAN PERSPECTIVES, ASPEN ANTHOLOGY, LA PRENSA LIBRE *(San José, Costa Rica),* LA PRENSA LITERARIA *(Managua, Nicaragua),* GREENFIELD RE-VIEW, NEW ORLEANS REVIEW, THIRD RAIL, NORTHWEST RE-VIEW, *and* ANTHOLOGY OF MAGAZINE VERSE & YEARBOOK OF AMERICAN POETRY, *In 1983, he received a Fulbright grant to translate poetry in Chile.*

In addition to Burning the Old Year, *his first volume of poetry, Mr. White has edited and translated two bilingual anthologies of Latin American poetry, both for Unicorn Press:* Poets of Nicaragua, 1916-1979, *which was published in 1982, and* Poets of Chile, 1965-1984, *which will be issued early in 1985.*

*Burning the Old Year has been
typeset in 11 point Baskerville by Polly Potter
and Rick Bruning. Inter-Collegiate Press
printed 1,000 copies on Plainwell's Natural
Neutral, an acid-free sheet which meets the
guidelines of the cpbgl of the Council on
Library Resources. All editions have been sewn
with linen thread.
Designed by Alan Brilliant.*